Body
of the
Great Bear

by
R.A. LAMB

R.A. Lamb

BOOK TWO OF ALASKAN FANTASY ADVENTURES IN THE IVORY BEAR SERIES

TABLE OF CONTENTS

TITLE PAGE

CHAPTER ONE

PROBLEMS

Alone the Alaskan Elder Weeok entered the one room cabin in the Arctic village of Barrow. A rush of frigid air caused the flame of the seal oil lamp next to Mark to flicker and cast dancing shadows on the walls.

The Elder spoke quietly, "Time for you return."

Mark stared into his black eyes. He started to speak but felt himself being drawn away. He knew he was returning to his other world.

Home safely from another Ivory Bear adventure Mark realized the challenges of living in two worlds were far from over.

In one he had moved to a new school in the middle of his freshman year. Here his problems began. Mark had no friends and was taunted by bullies as the new kid. He knew his troubles had just started and that one day he would be forced to face them. Pug and his buddies wouldn't leave him alone.

Later he accidentally stumbled into the second world when he walked into his

---

grandparents study to look for a book. He saw an ivory carving of a polar bear on the bookshelf and picked it up. The bear grew cold in his hand. Mark was transported to the wilderness of Alaska and into places which threatened his very existence.

He liked the thrill and challenge of the adventures. Mark wanted to tell someone what he had done but couldn't decide if he should. For now it would remain his secret. Time after time he returned to the ivory bear to take his mind away from the bullies.

Mark didn't know why he was chosen by the ivory bear or the power it controlled. He didn't realize yet that each adventure made him stronger and prepared him for the new challenges he would face in both worlds.

He finally made a friend at school. He and Michael Ling were about to share more than either could imagine.

CHAPTER TWO

PUG SETS A TRAP

Mark spent the weekend at his grandparents and the next morning at school was uneventful. There was just a hint of spring in the air. It was warm enough that neither Mark nor his new friend Michael wore jackets. After school that afternoon they walked across the sports field like they always did and couldn't help but notice the crowd at the edge of the cinder track.

Mark pointed, "Let's see what's going on."

They didn't know Pug had told his buddies, Rich and Greg, to spread the word that he was going to get Mark today. There were about three dozen classmates there to see the show. Pug stood in the center of the crowd and in a loud voice said, "That new kid is such a wimp. I'll bet he'll try to run but we won't let him. Right Rich?"

Rich and Greg snickered and so did a few others. Pug danced around like a prize fighter, jabbing the air and making sure everyone watched him.

He wore a T-shirt, faded knee length

cutoffs and sneakers and tugged at his ever present yellow ball cap. He wore it rally style with the bill pointing down his back.

It was too late when Mark realized what was happening. The crowd opened to let him and Michael into the center then closed around them. The trap was sprung.

Pug walked toward Mark and sneered, "Hey, sissy boy, I have sumpin' for ya." Pug made a fist.

Everyone else was quiet. Michael glanced at Mark and whispered, "What will we do?"

Mark didn't answer and stared directly at Pug. He watched the movement of Pug's eyes, the way the muscles twitched in the corner of Pug's mouth. Mark heard a voice in his mind, *Remember what the ivory bear has taught.*

Mark pictured the wrestling game in the snow with Ooluk at the Arctic village before the seal hunt. He could see him crouched with arms spread, ready to spring. He remembered all the moves Ooluk made. Of course, that was just in fun but Ooluk had said, "Marktok good."

Pug's eyes widened. He thought Mark would run, instead Mark stood his ground. Pug glanced around the crowd. They expected him to do something so he charged.

Mark remembered the stampede of the caribou and stepped quickly to the side as Pug lunged. Surprised, Pug grabbed nothing but air and stumbled to the ground. He jumped to his feet and whirled around.

Mark could see the fire in Pug's eyes like the fiery eyes of the grizzly. Just as Mark had done in Blacky Rustov's cabin on Kodiak Island, he charged.

"AAAAaah", he shouted and with an arm outstretched and his fist clinched, struck Pug in the center of his chest partially knocking the wind out of him.

Pug was now the hunted and he bent over and fought for breath. He slowly straightened. Mark could hear him try to inhale. It was a raspy, hollow sound. Pug moved toward Mark again. This time much slower. Not one of the class around the circle made a sound. Most stood frozen, wide-eyed with surprise, staring at Mark.

Mark crouched as Ooluk had crouched. He held his arms up as Ooluk had done, fingers opened and curled like the outstretched claws of the fighting bear.

Pug grasped at Mark's chest and grabbed the front of his shirt.

Mark closed his fingers into a fist and with a swing like the white bear on the ice pack hit Pug just above the ear. He heard Pug grunt at the impact, watched him shake his head and blink several times.

Rich looked shocked and glanced at Greg.

Pug partially lost his grip but held on.

Mark placed both hands over the one holding his shirt held tight and quickly bent forward.

Pug was forced downward, his bare knees crashed into the rough black cinders of the track. The sharp edges brought tears to

Pug's eyes. He lost his grip, grimaced and lowered his head.

Rich's and Greg's mouths hung open. They didn't seem to know what to say. It was over.

Mark slowly backed away but still kept his eyes directly on Pug. When he reached the edge of the crowd, it parted. He and Michael didn't look back. They continued home.

From then on Rich and Greg avoided Mark. When Pug saw him in the hallway at school he looked away and stared at the lock on his locker. He worked the combination until Mark was well past him. Pug didn't bother Mark again.

CHAPTER THREE

A SECRET SHARED

Mark asked his parents if he could invite Michael to Granddad's for the weekend. He grinned when they said yes and his mother suggested Michael come over Friday night so they could get an early start Saturday morning.

Michael arrived just after dinner with a backpack filled with clothes. The boys immediately went to Mark's room. It wasn't the neatest and the furniture didn't match but that didn't matter to either of them.

Mark told Michael to throw his pack on one of the twin beds and went to the closet to get a game. They played checkers and decided to call the third game a draw. They talked about school and sports and what they might do at Granddad's. Mark stared at the checkers and made a decision.

"Can you keep a secret?"

Michael's eyes lit up and nodded. Mark put his finger to his lips and walked to the closet.

He was there just a few seconds and came out holding the shoebox which contained his baseball cards, his rock collection and most importantly, the claw of the grizzly Blacky Rustov

11

had given him at Blacky's cabin on Kodiak Island.

They talked for a long time. Michael seemed to get more excited by the minute. They both jumped when they heard a knock on the door.

"Lights out boys."

Mark quickly put the lid on the shoebox, slid it under his bed and turned out the light. They lay in the darkness and continued to talk in low voices about mysteries, magic and sharing adventures.

The sun was shining through the bedroom window and Mark was the first of the two to wake. He woke Michael. Mom had breakfast ready. Oatmeal, juice, milk. Dad was outside and had the trunk of the car open. The boys finished breakfast and helped load. They were ready in record time. Mark and Michael climbed into the backseat and talked nonstop. When they arrived, Granddad was standing in the yard and they ran over to him.

"This is Michael."

Granddad reached out his hand and said, "Mark, show Michael around, then meet me in the backyard. I have something you can help me with."

The boys ran off toward the house and Granddad went to the car to greet the rest of the family. It didn't take long for the boys to find their way to the study. Mark guided Michael to the bookshelf. Michael's eyes widened and they both stared at the ivory bear. Mark heard Granddad calling "Need some help boys."

When they got outside, Granddad was coming out of the garage. He was carrying a large canvas bag and put it down by a stack of wooden stakes and poles. "Thought you might want to camp out tonight. You know, rough it."

Mark said, "That sounds great." He turned to Michael, "Help me spread the ground cloth."

Michael had a quizzical look but pitched in. "Why do you need this?"

"To keep moisture from seeping through the floor of the tent. Now help me put the tent over it and drive those pegs into the loops at the corners."

When that was done Granddad and Mark crawled inside and put the lodge pole in place. It looked like a wrestling match going on under the canvas. The tent took shape and the final stakes and tie ropes were secured.

Granddad brought out cots and sleeping bags. Mark and Michael put them inside and zipped the entrance closed. The boys stayed in the yard all afternoon. Every once in a while Michael would stop and stare at the house. Mark knew Michael was probably thinking about the ivory bear.

Everyone was hungry by dinnertime. Mark's mom and dad and his grandparents put on sweaters and gathered around the bar-b-que pit. The boys helped grill hamburgers. It was cool and getting dark when they finished. Everyone went inside and the grownups exchanged stories until bedtime.

Granddad got a battery powered lantern from the pantry and handed it to Mark, "If you outdoorsmen get too cold we'll leave the kitchen door unlocked." He winked at Mark and continued, "By the way, don't worry if you hear coyotes."

"Coyotes?" Michael said abruptly and glanced at Mark.

Mark took the lantern and in a serious voice replied, "We'll be careful."

The boys went to the tent. Mark opened the front flap, unzipped the doorway and went inside. He saw Michael look all around before entering.

Mark said, "Granddad was just joking. There are no coyotes around here."

He turned on the lantern and set it down between the two cots. They each unrolled a sleeping bag.

In a low voice Michael asked, "Will we have a chance to...? You know."

"I think so. Let's make sure everyone is asleep. Then we'll sneak into the study." Mark turned out the lantern, "It might look suspicious if we leave it on."

The boys crawled into their sleeping bags. They didn't zip them. They had no intention of going to sleep. Their excitement was too great. The night was quiet except for an occasional cricket and the wind which blew the tent flap. No use tying it down. They would be going inside soon. In whispers they tried to predict what the adventure might be.

Mark slipped out of his sleeping bag and quietly unzipped the front of the tent. Michael was right behind. Mark tied the front flap down and they slowly made their way toward the house. They didn't need the lantern. The half moon shining in the crisp night sky gave them enough light to get to the kitchen door. The only noise to be heard was the soft squeaking sound of their sneakers on the dew covered grass.

They crept inside. Everything was quiet. Mark and Michael slipped down the hallway to the study. As they entered, they heard the tick, tick of the grandfather clock in the corner. They eased over to the bookshelf. Mark felt his heart pound in his ears almost drowning out the tick of the clock and sensed Michael felt the same. Mark raised a finger to his lips, took hold of Michael's wrist then reached for the ivory bear.

Mark felt the familiar cold feeling. He saw Michael shiver. Mark had the sensation of moving downward, smelled fresh spruce and felt something cold brush across his back and face.

Michael's wrist was pulled from his grasp and they were separated. He quickly looked around to see where Michael had gone. He saw him ten feet below, stuck in a snow drift up to the sleeves of Michael's sealskin parka. The wolf ruff on his hood almost completely hid Michael's face. Mark could see only two dark eyes and a lock of black hair through the ring of gray fur.

Mark called out, "Are you all right?"

Michael waved his sealskin mitten and pushed his hood back with the other. "You are the one who has a problem."

Mark looked at his legs and for the first time realized he was sitting on a limb of a pine tree well above the ground. The bough was covered with snow. He pushed the hood of his parka back with his mitten and looked upward. He could see the path of his descent through the snow covered branches which had brushed against him. The ivory bear had permitted Michael to come along.

Mark looked around. They were in a dense pine and spruce forest. Everything looked very much the same in all directions. There were large snow covered trees and the ground was covered with snow except for a few large rocks which the wind swept bare. He pointed at two animal skin backpacks on the ground not far from Michael. "See if there is a rope in one of the packs."

Michael struggled to get free of the snow bank and almost lost a mukluk. He succeeded in pulling the caribou skin boot back on and worked himself free. He waded through the deep snow to the packs.

Michael pulled off his mittens. They dangled from leather thongs which were tied to his parka. He reached for a coil of braided leather rope tied to the side of one of the packs.

Michael blew on his fingers and untied it. He threw the rope up to Mark. After several tries Mark caught it. He tied one end around his waist and looped the other around a branch just over his head. This let the rope dangle to the ground below.

He took hold of the rope with both mittens and carefully moved so he could wrap his legs around the trunk, then eased himself off the branch. Mark held on tight as he let the rope slowly slide through his mittens and lowered himself to the ground. His caribou hide pants and mukluks kept him from getting scraped by the trunk on his descent. He let himself drop the last few feet falling into a soft drift of snow. Mark smiled at Michael as he untied the rope and coiled it once more. "I guess we better get started."

"What do we do now?" inquired Michael.

"Put on one of the backpacks and let's try to find out where we are. When we do we'll take it from there," Mark got up. He brushed the snow off his parka and pants and trudged over to a pack.

He found it was laying on something they would need if they were going to find a way out. Snowshoes. He picked one up. The frame was made of birch and the webbing of knotted rawhide. There was a leather strap to tie it to his mukluk. Mark put the snowshoes on and tried to walk.

They did keep him from sinking into the snow but he stepped on the edge of the other shoe and fell. They both laughed and Mark discovered that by swinging his feet to the outside as he stepped forward it worked a lot better.

Mark looked in his pack and found a folding hunting knife, strips of dried meat, some dried tundra grass and a black flint pebble.

He also found several rawhide laces, some leather pouches filled with dried leaves and tiny flowers and an old aluminum pot among other things.

He used the knife to cut down two pine saplings just above the snow line and about as big around as the handle of a baseball bat. It took some work and he cut and trimmed them so they were just longer than they were tall. Mark handed one to Michael and said, "Take a walking stick. It will help you keep your balance." Mark and Michael practiced walking in the snowshoes before putting on the packs.

Mark nodded, "Let's get started. We need to find shelter before it gets any darker."

"Which way do we go, Mark?"

"Hmm. This way." He wasn't really sure which way but someone had to choose. The only sound they heard was the crunching sound of the snow under their snowshoes. There was no wind. The forest was still. Overhead clouds blanketed the sky. Mark recognized them. They were gray storm clouds. Light snow began to fall.

Mark said, "The Eskimos call this qa-na."

"What's that?"

"Falling snow."

"Where did you learn Eskimo?"

"I learned a few words from a book in the school library. Let's go."

After walking for what seemed like hours they stopped to rest. Michael saw some tracks and bent over for a closer look. He motioned to Mark, "See those dog tracks, maybe there are people nearby."

Mark looked at them. There were at least three sets and they were larger than a husky would make. He didn't say anything but he was convinced these were the tracks of Alaskan wolves.

They walked and rested, walked and rested through the silent forest. The snow continued to fall. The flakes got bigger. Once in a while a branch became overloaded and bent enough so that the collection of snow cascaded to the ground.

They came to a rock cliff. It was four times as high as they were tall and angled outward offering some shelter from the falling snow. Some large boulders lay on the ground on one side. They must have broken loose and slumped forward. This created a two sided windbreak and the ground beneath had only a light covering of snow. The evening light was fading and with it the weather seemed to get colder.

Mark said, "Let's stop here for the night."

Michael turned toward Mark and had a funny look on his face. Mark let his pack slide to the ground inside the edge the windbreak. His shoulders ached and he was happy to feel some relief. He took off his snowshoes and leaned them against the rock wall. Michael did likewise.

"Do you mean we are not going back to your Granddad's? We're going to stay here tonight?"

Mark smiled and nodded as he scraped the thin covering of snow from the undergrowth with his mukluk. The ground was covered with a layer of pine needles and twigs.

He said, "Scrape off as much snow as you can and make a pile of the needles here." He unfolded his knife and cut some dead branches from nearby spruce and pine trees, brought an armload back and set them beside the pile of needles and twigs. Mark broke some small limbs into pieces.

Snap. He broke a branch. "Good." he said out loud, "It's dry."

Michael watched as Mark cleared a fire ring several feet from the rock wall and on the edge of the windbreak.

"Why don't you make the fire up against the cliff?"

"Because we want to put our backs against the wall and let the fire reflect its heat off the rocks. Besides if a bear comes along you'd want the fire between us and the bear wouldn't you?"

"A bear?"

"You never know."

Mark removed his mittens and took some of the needles and twigs and put them in the center of the cleared area. He opened his pack and took out a small handful of dry tundra grass and placed it on the needles. He got the black flint pebble and opened his knife. Patiently he struck the rock with the back of the knife blade. A spark flew to the dry grass, another and another. A wisp of smoke. He pushed back the hood of his parka, leaned down and gently blew. More smoke, a tiny glow, a flame.

Mark quickly added small branches, then a few more pine needles and twigs. He continued to gently blow on the flame. The fire erupted. Michael stood silently as Mark added more of the branches he'd gathered.

Mark said, "Would you get the pot and

pack it with snow?"

The fire burned brightly, the flames casting flickering shadows on the cliff wall. The boys felt its warmth and relaxed. Mark put the pan of snow on some glowing embers. As the snow melted, he added more. Soon a curl of steam rose from the water. He took a few pinches of dried leaves and tundra flowers from a leather pouch and put them in the hot water. Michael found tin cups in his pack. Mark filled them from the pot. The boys squatted next to the rock wall sipping the bittersweet taste of tundra tea and biting off pieces from strips of dried meat.

Mark put more branches on the fire and they stared at the flames until their eyes drooped and they drifted off to sleep. Michael was the first to wake. He nudged Mark and both uncurled their legs. Mark's muscles were stiff as he stood.

The fire had almost gone out. Michael added some small branches and blew on the embers as he had seen Mark do and filled the pan with snow. After a breakfast of meat and tea, they discussed what to do next.

Mark walked to the edge of the windbreak and looked at the heavy gray clouds. More snow was on the way.

His eyes scanned the forest. Their snowshoe tracks had been covered by fresh snow. No one knew or would discover they were there. He lowered his head considering what to do next and stared at the blanket of white. His eyes focused on a set of tracks only a few steps from where they had slept.

There in the fresh snow, at the edge of their windbreak, was a clear set of paw prints. Whatever it was had watched them as they slept. It was clear they must be more careful.

They needed to leave and find a trapper's cabin, a native village or they would run out of food, run out of energy and freeze to death in the lonely forest. A gentle wind wafted the smell of the campfire to Mark's nose. He recognized the smell of spruce. Mark turned and said, "We must start walking but first we need weapons."

Michael's eyes stared at Mark in amazement and said, "Why? What?"

Mark said, "I read an article about an Eskimo hunter whose rifle jammed and was useless. He made a spear as his ancient ancestors had done. That's what we are going to do."

There was a hint of fear in Michael's voice as he said, "How are we going to do that?"

"Put the tip of your walking stick in the fire. Let it burn for a few minutes then rub the burning tip against this rock wall. We'll need to do that several times until we have worn the tip to a sharp point. They will be our walking spears."

Mark and Michael put the tips into the flame. Soon the wall was streaked with black marks from the walking spears. They put out the fire, put on their snowshoes and packs and walked into the trees. Mark broke trail, Michael followed. Mark didn't think Michael had seen the paw prints.

They continued the pattern of walking and

resting as they had done the day before, however their rest periods were getting longer. They came to a break in the trees. It was about twenty steps wide and cut an open trail through the forest to their right and to their left. Both boys recognized it as a stream, frozen solid under its wintry coat of snow. They crossed and walked into the forest on the other side and continued walking, searching for help of any kind. After what seemed like hours they came upon a second break in the trees.

"Another stream," Michael called to Mark. They crossed it and moved on. It was getting late in the afternoon, what light there was began to fade. Mark stopped and turned to Michael. Mark was breathing hard, "We better look for a place to camp. Let me know if you see anything."

Michael nodded. Mark was feeling a little light headed but didn't mention it. While he had eaten mouthfuls of snow he didn't realize he was becoming dehydrated from the freezing weather and their exertions. He wondered if Michael felt the same.

They trudged on. Mark called, "There are some rocks."

When they got there they both stared unbelievingly at what they saw. On the rock wall were the black marks from their walking spears.

They had no choice and again made camp in the windbreak. Mark cleared away the ashes from the previous night's fire and gathered pine needles and twigs. For the first time he felt the pangs of fear. He fought against it, his vision became blurry. Mark inhaled deeply. The cold air hurt his throat and chest. He must not show this weakness to Michael. They would find help.

He went to cut some dead branches. On his way he saw the two sets of shoe prints they had made that morning and cutting across them were at least three sets of large paw prints following their trail.

He again made a fire. This time Michael was more help. Mark showed Michael the paw prints, and while they ate they decided to take turns staying awake and keeping the fire burning. Mark gathered more branches.

He took off his mittens and searched through his backpack until he found the rawhide laces. Mark noticed they only had enough dried meat strips for two more meals. He opened his hunting knife and tied the handle to the end of the walking spear with the rawhide lace. Whoever was on guard would at least have a sharp weapon.

Michael said, "I'll take the first watch."

That was fine with Mark. He really felt tired and curled up next to the cliff wall.

A few hours later Mark was awakened by the distant howl of an Alaskan wolf. He took his turn and Michael tried to sleep.

Some hours later the fire had all but gone out. Mark sat cross-legged on the ground, his head drooped, and the knife spear lay across his lap.

He came fully awake and his mittens tightly grasped the spear when he heard the guttural growl of the lone wolf not three steps from where he sat.

Mark slowly raised his head until he could make out the wolf's form through the ruff of the hood of his parka. Yellow eyes were squarely watching him. The wolf snarled, baring his white fangs and sharp ripping teeth. He was larger than Mark anticipated, weighing almost as much as he did. Shiny black fur covered the head and snout. The rest of the wolf's body was silvery gray.

Their eyes locked. Mark saw the wolf's haunches tense and swung his spear as the wolf lunged catching its right shoulder with the knife blade cutting a deep gash and deflecting the charge.

The wolf with the black head landed in the smoldering embers of the fire, sending a spray of sparks into the air. The wolf tried to get to his feet and stumbled on its wounded limb. Mark could smell the distinctive odor of singed fur.

As though the world were suddenly in slow motion, Mark stared as the wolf turned on three legs and vanished into the trees leaving a trail of red in the white snow.

Several other pairs of eyes watched from the shadows, then followed their leader into the forest.

Michael sat frozen but not from the cold. He appeared shocked by the scene which had just unfolded in front of him. Mark's heart pumped madly. There could be no thought of sleep now. Mark rebuilt the fire with the last of the branches. It was beginning to get lighter. They ate in silence and broke camp, neither wanted to talk about the danger they'd escaped.

As they pulled on their packs, Mark said, "I have an idea but you can choose the way if you want."

Michael said, "I really don't know Mark, you lead."

Mark headed along yesterday's trail. At their first rest stop he said, "I'm heading toward the stream we crossed. It may lead us to help. I just don't know if we should go right or left when we get there."

Snow was beginning to fall. The flakes were big and would soon cover their old trail. They walked as fast as they could but their old tracks were vanishing. Mark stopped and lined up the last prints he could see with a distant tree some thirty paces ahead. From there they would have to guess. When they reached the tree Mark thought he could see a break in the forest ahead. They had reached the stream.

The boys were relieved and let their packs slip to the ground. Mark opened his and withdrew the last two strips of dried meat. They discussed which way to go. Right or left. There was no way to tell with the stream frozen. You couldn't tell upstream from downstream.

Mark said, "Maybe the ivory bear will help us choose the way." And he set the butt end of his knife spear upright on the ice.

Michael watched. Mark let go of the spear. It remained upright for a moment then fell to the left.

Michael said, "I'm ready, let's go."

The boys followed the clearing cut by the stream. *If a trapper or a village was somewhere nearby, they would probably be on a stream,* Mark thought, but he didn't know if it was true.

The snow got heavier and the wind started to blow. In the forest the wind was not as noticeable but on the open streambed it gusted and blew swirls of snow around their legs.

It drifted in several places and it was harder to move forward than the boys anticipated. Snowfall got so heavy they could only see a few feet in front of them. Mark stopped beside a drift and put his hood to Michael's. He shouted above the wind. "We can't go much farther. Help me dig a snow cave."

Mark took off his snowshoes and used one as a shovel. He dug into the drift. Michael took off his snowshoes and helped. They dug a hole in the side of the drift big enough for them and their packs.

They crawled inside and put their packs to the entrance as a barrier against the swirling wind. At least they were out of the blinding snow.

"This can't last long," Mark said, but he wasn't sure. The storm blew well into the night. The boys remained huddled together in the snow cave until morning. They had no more food. There was no way to make a fire. All they had for their morning meal was a few handfuls of snow. Mark looked at Michael and saw the fatigue in his eyes. The entrance of their cave had completely drifted over.

This is almost like the igloo on the ice pack, Mark thought. He pushed the backpacks outward. Snow cascaded into the entrance. The boys crawled out and were greeted by a gust of freezing wind. It was still snowing. The flakes were smaller but visibility was poor. At their feet the wind swirled the fallen snow like shifting sand. Above the gray-white storm clouds filled the sky, to either side was an endless snowy forest. They wearily put on their snowshoes, packs and holding their walking spears walked headfirst into the blowing storm.

Without food and little rest every movement was an effort. Their pace grew slower, the rests more frequent. Mark could no longer feel his feet. At midday Michael called weakly to Mark, "Let's sit down for awhile. I'm so tired."

Mark knew the signs. If they stopped too long they might never get up. It was so easy in the intense cold to just sit down and go to sleep. A sleep from which you never wake.

He said, "Okay but just a few minutes."

Michael stumbled and fell. He didn't make any attempt to get up or slip off the pack. Mark walked back to him and pulled on the sleeve of his parka. Michael's eyes were closed.

"Don't go to sleep. You must stay awake. If you don't you might... I mean you must stay awake."

Michael eyelids fluttered and he squinted up at Mark, "Just a little while." And he closed his eyes. The swirling snow began to pile against Michael's legs.

Mark pulled off Michael's pack. They would leave it here. He put his arm around Michael's hood and pulled him to his knees. "Just walk to the edge of the trees. Mark struggled to get Michael to his feet. Mark shouted, "Michael. Where is your mitten?"

One of Michael's hands was bare. It was bluish white. Mark panicked. It must have come off when he fell. Mark went to his knees and searched the snow. He found it. The thong tying Michael's mitten to his parka had broken in the fall. Mark took off his own mittens and slipped Michael's back on. Slowly they made their way to the trees leaving behind a backpack now almost covered beneath the blowing snow.

Once inside the forest the wind eased, the trees acted as a windbreak. Mark again took off his mittens and with numb fingers retied Michael's mitten to his parka. He took off his pack and untied the leather rope. He tied one end around Michael's waist. He tied the other end around himself.

Now as he broke trail he would know if Michael fell. They slowly moved forward within the line of trees keeping the streambed in view. It was their compass.

Mark drove himself, *Just another few steps, another few steps.*

The stream widened dramatically. The snowfall had slowed and the wind eased. The boys struggled with their last energy to the trees edge. In the waning afternoon light they saw that the stream entered a frozen lake. Mark guessed it was maybe five hundred steps across. And on the other side Mark could make out the shapes of half-a-dozen shacks with curls of smoke coming from their chimneys.

"A village," he rasped, his throat dry, "We

found it."

Mark turned to Michael, grasped his arm and hoarsely shouted. "A village."

Out of breath, the boys stood on the study carpet and stared at one another. Mark let go of Michael's wrist and put the ivory bear back in its place.

CHAPTER FOUR

FIRE MOUNTAIN

The boys quietly made their way back to their tent in Granddad's backyard. They crouched and went through the entrance. Mark lowered the front flap and zipped the door closed. They sat on their cots and stared at each other.

Michael broke the silence, "That was awesome. Can we do that again?"

"Are you sure you want to? Weren't you scared?"

"Yes, it was better than riding the Red Devil roller coaster at the fairgrounds. Can we do it again?"

"Sure if you want to. We'll go to the study after breakfast." They crawled into their sleeping bags and fell into a deep sleep.

They both woke to a sound. Zzzzzip. Granddad poked his head through the door of the tent, "Are you two going to sleep all day? Breakfast is almost ready."

Michael rubbed his eyes and Mark stretched. "We'll be right there", Mark said as he began getting out of his sleeping bag.

The boys had slept in their clothes and were ready to walk to the house with Granddad. They sat down at the kitchen table.

"See any coyotes last night?" Granddad said and winked at Mark's dad.

Michael said without thinking, "No sir, we saw something better than that. Err, what I mean is ..."

Mark broke in, "Ah you mean your dream?"

"Yeah, I mean in my dream, ah, last night." Michael's voice drifted off and he took a bite of scrambled eggs.

Granddad grinned. No one else seemed to notice. Mark helped clear the dishes and put them in the sink. He turned to Michael, "Do you want to go down to the creek and look for turtles?"

Michael tried to sound enthusiastic, "Sure, that would be great."

"First," Mark said, "there's something I want to show you in Granddad's study."

Michael's eyes brightened, "Okay." And he got up from his chair.

Granddad watched intently as the boys hurried down the hallway, then turned and continued talking to Mark's mom and dad.

Mark whispered, "Hold onto my arm." And with the other he reached toward the bookshelf. Mark saw Michael shiver.

Mark felt the wind; his vision was out of focus. He felt Michael let go of his arm and Mark slowly scanned their surroundings.

There was the sound of birds in trees, the

smell of pine and spruce. There was the feel of solid ground underfoot. Then for a few seconds he felt a vibration. It caused Mark to look down. He saw they were standing on a well traveled path which wound through a dense forest. The boughs filtered the morning sunlight. A gentle breeze moved the treetops causing the mixture of shadow and light to dance on the ground. Mark looked up and saw the dark gray peaks of mountains some distance from where they stood.

The boys were dressed the same, high topped moccasins tied to their lower legs with strips of leather, wool pants and heavy plaid flannel shirts. Mark's was red and black. Michael's was blue and white. The exception was a small leather pouch tied around Mark's waist. In it he felt a familiar shape. He suddenly felt more confident as his hand firmly grasped the folding hunting knife.

Off the path, the floor of the forest was covered with brown pine needles with a few sprigs of greenery here and there. Mark walked to a tree beside the path and cut off a strip of bark. *As the grizzly marked his territory, I'll mark our starting point,* he thought

The path sloped gently downward to their left. The boys didn't hesitate. They started walking down the path looking from side to side, watching and listening for movements on the forest floor.

Mark broke the silence, "If we are going to find water, we'll probably find it in a valley."

Michael nodded.

They walked for some time and came to a clearing filled with low growing bushes. Ahead they could see the path began to go slightly uphill. The clearing was shaped like a saucer filled with marsh grass and low woody undergrowth. Mark took a step into it and his moccasin sank into the peaty bottom. Water oozed over the top of his foot. He looked closer at the bushes. There were red berries. He picked some, studied them for a moment and popped them in his mouth. They were juicy and had a familiar tangy taste.

"Cranberries", he said, "lunch."

He and Michael picked and ate. The juicy berries filled their stomachs and quenched their thirst. Mark continued to pick berries and filled his pouch. He didn't know when they would find more food. The boys sat down to rest under a tree. The forest was still. A few clouds began to gather and a light rain started to fall. Mark was sure this afternoon shower wouldn't last long. The boys sat and talked in low voices in the gently falling rain.

Mark caught a glimpse of movement across the clearing and stood. Both he and Michael jumped at the sound of something big splashing through the muskeg marsh. It disappeared into the forest.

"Wow, a moose," said Michael "I've never seen anything that big."

"I must have scared her when I stood up." Mark's eyes were as big as saucers. "Let's move."

The shower stopped. They continued

along the trail. It seemed now to be winding around a hill to their right. A narrow streambed, four steps wide crossed the path just ahead. The boys stopped to look. It carried only a trickle of water. The rocks were heavily stained with yellow, white and reddish brown streaks. Mark cupped his hand, scooped up some water and held it to his nose. It smelled funny. He detected the slight odor of rotten eggs.

Michael said, "Where do you think the stains come from, a mine? Maybe there's a gold mine up there."

"One way to find out," Mark replied. And he started walking up the slope beside the steam. Within fifty paces the hill got steeper. The boys had to hold onto tree trunks as they climbed. Then the ground leveled out for awhile and rose abruptly into a cliff of dark gray rock. The stained streambed led to a small pool of water at the base of the cliff and mist hung over it like a shroud.

As they approached, the boys noticed the air temperature was warmer. Mark crouched beside the pool, held his hand above the surface for a moment and lowered it into the water. "This is really warm, must be a hot spring," Mark said. "How about a dip in our own hot tub?"

Michael grinned and was already unbuttoning his flannel shirt. Naked as jay birds the boys stepped into the water. It had a sloping rocky bottom and was waist deep toward the center.

The deeper they went the hotter it got so the boys moved until they found a spot at just the right temperature. They sat and talked about their adventure so far, the fun they were having and what they might find next. They relaxed in the warm water.

Suddenly it got hotter. Ripples formed on the surface of the pool. The rocks they were sitting on started to vibrate.

"Hey," Michael shouted and they got out as quickly as they could. The boys stood at the edge of the pool and watched as the water bubbled up and overflowed into the adjacent streambed. They smelled the strong odor of rotten eggs and the ground began to shake under their feet.

Small rocks fell from the cliff above. It was hard to stand and they held onto the side of the cliff wall. The trees swayed vigorously and pine needles fell like green rain. It lasted less than a minute, and stopped.

They heard a rumble in the distance. Michael stared at Mark, "Was that thunder?" A few bubbles burst on the surface of the water.

Mark shouted, "Get your clothes and get away from the pool." The boys grabbed their things and moved to the edge of the trees. Steaming water spouted as high as Mark was tall from the center of their natural hot tub.

Dripping wet, and clutching their clothes, the boys watched their peaceful world change around them. The distant rumbling stopped.

The pool's surface quieted and their world returned except for the carpet of green pine needles covering the forest's floor.

Michael asked, "What was that?"

Mark excitedly replied, "An earthquake and now I know why the spring was hot. That rumbling in the mountains might be from a volcano."

"Wow, do you think it's going to erupt?"

"I don't know but let's get out of here."

They quickly dressed and made their way to the path below. Water was still running in the stained streambed. They crossed to the other side and looked ahead. About twenty steps from them the path split into two paths. A large cedar log, carved and painted, about four times as tall as Mark, stood upright in the ground. They stopped in their tracks and stared. Mark said in a low voice, "A totem pole. See the animals carved on it?"

"Yeah, the one with the red and blue face looks like a bear.

Mark said, "The one above it may be a wolf. And the black one at the top looks like a crow."

Michael looked puzzled, "What does it mean?"

"I don't know, but it's a sign that Indians were here or are here."

"They're friendly, aren't they?"

"I don't know. I hope so."

One path looked well traveled; the other had some fallen branches across it and in places was covered with leaves and pine needles.

Mark looked serious, "Until we know if the people are friendly, I think we should explore the path which looks abandoned."

Michael looked surprised, "Okay, if that's

what you want to do, let's go."

The boys watched their step and headed down the abandoned trail. It was easy enough to follow even though it was cluttered with debris. They stopped to rest. Michael sat down and leaned against the trunk of a tall pine.

Mark looked intently at the trunk and slowly turned to study the others around them. He said, "That's odd."

Michael looked up, "What's that?"

"The older trees are charred," he pointed at the trunk above Michael's head. "And the smaller trees and undergrowth are not. I'll bet there was a fire through here. I wonder what started it."

Suddenly the earth shook, not hard, but noticeably. They heard distant rumbling again. The boughs of the trees swayed. The needles made a swishing sound in the air, some falling to the forest floor.

Michael got to his feet. The black smudge on the back of his plaid shirt would remind them of this place. They continued onward. Mark and Michael felt more vibrations.

The path wound its way upward toward the base of a very steep rocky hill with a flat top. It was barren of trees. The only living things on it were a few gnarled bushes that grew in the crags of the rocks. The path they were following ended at the foot of the cliff. The boys looked up. The hill seemed to be made of a bundle of vertical columns of dense, dark rock. Some were broken and pieces lay around them on the ground. The cross section of the columns had a polygonal shape. *Strange*, thought Mark, *is this natural or something else?*

It looked like the broken columns formed a staircase spiraling to the top. Mark looked at Michael and went first. There were lots of loose rocks and they carefully watched their step as they climbed. When they finally reached the top the boys discovered others had been there before them. Five totems forming the corners of a large pentagon stood watch. Mark thought, *each is topped with the carving of a crow. I wonder why?*

Mark heard a voice in his mind, *Beware of the Raven*. He didn't tell Michael.

There were several large flat rocks within the perimeter of the totems. Some had bundles lying on them. The boys went over to one. An end was ripped open. They stared in shock. In it was a human skeleton and they were looking at its skull. The bundle was longer than either boy was tall. It was wrapped in animal skins and tied with strips of leather. Blue, red and yellow patterns were painted on the skins.

Mark whispered, "A burial ground. We should leave."

Mark looked around. The flat topped peak they were standing on was several times higher than the tallest tree below. For the first time they could see the black conical shaped mountains in the distance standing in stark contrast to the green canopy of the pine forest. A cloud of steam hung over one of the peaks. The mountain suddenly blew a glowing white column of steam and debris high into the afternoon sky.

Within seconds they heard a whoosh like the wind before a storm and claps like thunder.

As though struck by a giant lighting bolt, the earth shook as it released its energy from within. The shaking moved loose rocks around them and the leather wrapped bundle at their feet. The skull spilled out from its resting place and rolled to a stop between Mark's moccasins. He couldn't breathe. On instinct Mark raised both arms, his palms outward. We mean no harm, his mind shouted.

Shadows passed across the ground. Both boys' eyes were drawn skyward. They saw the gleaming black bodies and spread wings of ravens, circling above. The birds screeched a warning as each swooped downward.

One barely missed Michael's head and thumped his shoulder with its wing. The ravens seemed intent upon driving the young intruders from this place. The boys quickly turned and started their descent.

"Be careful Michael. Don't slip."

A misstep could mean disaster, Mark thought, as he reached for a handhold. It gave way, clamoring downward sending a shower of smaller rocks cascading to the ground far below.

Again and again the ravens dived, screeching and beating at Mark and Michael with their wings. It seemed like an eternity before the boys reached the safety of the ground. Mark quickly stooped to picked up a rock and threw it over his shoulder at his tormentors as he and Michael ran into the cover of the forest.

They ran until Mark's lungs burned. Out of

breath and covered with sweat they sank to their knees beside a fallen tree. Gasping for air the boys raised their heads above the trunk to search the horizon. The ravens had given up their pursuit and rose again to perch atop the burial mountain.

There was more thunderous noise and shaking. The sky began to dim as a gray cloud of dust from the volcano blanketed the forest and dampened the sun. The white ash filtered through the tree tops and coated the boughs. Mark caught some in his hand. It felt gritty. "An eruption, its beginning," he said to Michael. "We must hurry."

The other path, Mark thought. The boys ran back along the path they'd traveled. They paid no attention to the fallen branches and other debris which littered the trail. The rain of white ash filled the air and covered the forest floor.

They arrived at the totem where the other trail joined. It now stood coated in a veil of white. Mark looked at the carved raven at the top. He said to himself, *It's watching us.*

The boys turned down the traveled path. The rumbling continued. The air was now a dense cloud, making it hard to see very far ahead. They cupped their hands over their noses to keep from choking. Mark glanced at Michael. His hair, his face and shirt were white. He left white footprints on the path which soon would vanish as more ash fell. *He looks like something from the spirit world,* Mark thought.

There was no time to rest. Mark's legs

burned. I can't go much farther but we must keep moving.

His eyes stung and watered, blurring his vision. He shouted to Michael, "Don't get separated. Stay together."

He caught a whiff of wood smoke. Mark remembered the charred trunks in the forest. The boys heard loud popping behind them. It got louder, like the cracks of rifle shots. They stopped to look back and saw a glow through the cloud of ash.

A forest fire. Sap filled trunks, superheated and turned to steam, exploded and echoed through the forest as the fire raged, advancing closer and closer.

Mark thought, *nothing can survive this. Not trees, not animals....* He glanced back.

Something big was running along the path and rapidly gaining on them. Instinctively he pushed Michael sideways and out of the way. They rolled, stirring up a cloud of white dust as a bear ran past them. They heard its labored panting as it raced ahead and disappeared into the curtain of falling ash. Only its snout was black the rest of its body coated white like everything else in the forest.

Mark said to himself, we've got to keep going. He helped Michael get to his feet. Behind them they could see the fire advancing, consuming everything in its path. For the first time they felt the heat from the approaching inferno.

"We can't stop. Our only chance is to keep running." Mark shouted.

The once green tree tops over their heads burst into flame. Burning needles rained down like a thousand sparklers. The fire was winning.

Michael stumbled and fell behind. Mark turned and shouted, "Michael keep up." The roar of the fire drowned out his voice.

Swirling smoke and raging fire. The inferno was generating its own wind. Sucking air inward, feeding the flames.

Mark retraced his steps. His eyes burned. He brushed glowing pine needles from his hair. Michael was on his knees on the path, coughing. Trees and undergrowth were now ablaze on either side of them. Mark grabbed Michael's arm and pulled him up. Michael staggered forward. Mark called upon every ounce of energy he had.

It hurt to breathe. Mark's chest pounded as they stumbled ahead. They entered a clearing. The path widened. Log houses, totem poles. A deserted village now in flames. Mark glanced upward. On top of a totem, a raven with its outstretched wings on fire stared down at them. Ahead, through the clouds of smoke they saw a rushing stream at the edge of the village.

Mark thought, *Water. An escape.* He grabbed Michael's flannel shirt and they fell into the current. They held onto each other. Coughing. Sputtering. The rushing water carrying them faster and faster downstream and away from the flames.

Ahead was another sound. The roar of rapids. Mark could see the white water rush around large jagged rocks in the raging stream. They narrowly missed being smashed into a boulder. They were at the current's mercy, bobbing like corks as they entered the rapids. White water foamed around them and over them. They gasped for breath. Coughing and choking they held onto each other. Exhausted Mark heard a voice in his mind, *Persevere, swim to survive.*

Ahead he saw the water disappear over a fall. Before that an eddy pool was swirling. Mark shouted, "Kick Michael, swim, kick."

With their last energy they kicked and caught by the swirl of the eddy were pushed toward the bank. Behind a protective boulder, in quiet water they lay half submerged, no energy left to drag themselves onshore.

Hair singed, faces blackened with soot and bodies bruised, they crawled out of the stream. They had outrun the fire and survived the raging water.

Mark and Michael lay outstretched for a long time on the bank trying to regain some strength.

Mark had an idea, What if I... He looked at Michael, "Hold onto my arm." Mark made a fist with his other hand as though holding something and raised it to his forehead. "Return," he whispered. He felt the wind, his vision lost focus. Then it cleared.

There was the tick of the pendulum clock. The feel of carpet beneath his feet. Mark looked around. Shelves of books, a desk, a chair.

He said to Michael, "We told Granddad we were going to the creek to look for turtles."

Michael said,"Uh, huh."

They closed the study door behind them.

CHAPTER FIVE

ARCTIC CAVERN

The car was packed after breakfast the next morning and everyone said goodbye. Michael thanked Mark's grandparents, "It's a weekend I'll never forget."

As Mark opened the car door to get into the back seat, Granddad handed him a small box, "Just something I wanted you to have."

Dad said, "Everybody in? Goodbye, see you soon."

Granddad smiled, nodded and took a step back into the yard as the car slowly backed down the gravel driveway and turned onto the street. As it started to pick up speed Mark looked out the rear window. He saw Granddad watching them drive away, one arm raised his palm facing outward. Even though they were too far away for Granddad to see, Mark raised one hand palm facing outward, toward the road behind them. For a moment he felt deep sadness and didn't understand why. He turned around and settled into his seat for the long ride home.

Michael was looking out the side window at the passing scenery. In the front seat Mark's mom and dad were watching the road ahead. Mark couldn't wait any longer. He eased the top off the box Granddad had given him. A sealed envelope was folded on top. Under it was a soft leather pouch a little larger than Mark's hand.

He glanced around without moving his head. No one was paying any attention. Mark eased the pouch out of the box. There were several white dots painted on it. Four of the dots formed the corners of a rectangle and three more formed a crooked line off one corner. What could that be, he asked himself? His heart began to beat faster as he pulled back the leather flap and looked inside.

Mark caught his breath and his gaze shot to the front seat. His mom and dad were still looking at the road ahead. He saw his mother turn and say something to his dad but it was mixed with the hum of the tires on the road and he couldn't make out what she said. He glanced at Michael who was still looking out the side window.

As if in slow motion, Mark reached out and took hold of Michael's arm to get his attention. Michael slowly turned his head. Mark could no longer hear the hum of the tires. Mark's hand grew cold. He saw only darkness.

The boys were no longer in the back seat but found themselves standing inside the mouth of a cave. They stared out at the rain and glanced upward at black low hanging clouds covering the mountain tops like a veil.

Rain mixed with sleet was pummeling the ground. A cold Arctic wind gusted causing the tundra grass a few feet away to whip about like waves on a restless sea.

Mark could see a path leading away from the cave's entrance. It looked well trodden by years of use. *I'll bet hunters took shelter here*, he thought.

A short distance away, the path disappeared into the mist and pounding storm. The rain puddled at their feet and splashed icy water on their mukluks.

The boys turned and stepped into the relative dryness of the cavern. The dim light from the entrance allowed them to see some of their surroundings. The walls, floor and ceiling were gray limestone.

Immediately to their right they saw a fire ring strewn with ashes and charred pieces of wood. Between it and the cavern wall was a pile of animal bones, the remains of past meals perhaps, discarded over the years by the many hunters who had camped here.

To the left was a stack of dry wood and grass. Beside that were hundreds of broken pieces of flint scattered about. Mark had read about the Alaskan natives who followed migrating herds in the tundra covered valleys along the Brooks Range, north of the Arctic Circle, He turned to Michael, "I think this is a hunting camp."

"What do you mean?"

"See those piles of sharp rock chips? It's called a chipping ground. It's where the hunters made arrowheads and spear points. They carried pieces of flint with them and made the tips when they needed them."

Michael stared at the piles of flint and moved pieces about with the toe of his sealskin mukluk. "Look at this." He kneeled and picked up a piece of flint chipped in the shape of a spear head with the tip broken off.

"Hang onto that," Mark said, "It may come in handy."

They could see no deeper into the cavern. It felt damp, cold and the air smelled musty and stale. Mark raised his hand to his belt and felt the familiar leather pouch and folding knife. He placed a few small branches and a handful of dry grass in the fire ring. With flint and steel he lighted a fire and placed some larger branches on it.

Outside the storm raged. Rain turned to snow, the wind howled. The fire's heat relieved the cold damp feeling and the flames lighted more of the cavern. The boys looked around.

On the ceiling the smoke of many fires had blackened a large circular area. Curiously the smoke didn't accumulate and fill the cave. It disappeared, possibly being drawn to the outside by cracks in the limestone.

Michael took a few steps into the cavern. He crouched and touched one of several rolls of caribou hides.

He called out, "This must be a sleeping area. Here are some sleeping skins. And here are some clubs leaning against the wall." He picked one up and carried it toward the fire ring and handed it to Mark.

The club was about three feet long and

one end had a glob of something black and sticky. Mark touched it. He held his fingers to his nose. "Tar," Mark said, "they're torches, not clubs." He held it to the fire and it immediately burst into a smoky ball of yellow flame. Mark held the torch high as he and Michael explored the recesses of the cavern. On the wall above the sleeping skins hung a leather pouch filled with dried meat and another filled with dried berries.

They continued walking to the left in a circle around the cavern wall. Mark looked up and saw a smoke blackened line on the roof leading from the fire ring to the far corner. "Michael look over there, a tunnel." Both stood in awe at the dark tunnel in front of them. "Grab another torch and follow me," Mark said as he entered its mouth.

Holding his torch high he could see the trail of black soot on the roof of the cave. *Many have been this way before*, Mark thought. The cave was straight for twenty steps then turned to the right. They walked another twenty-five steps and the cave widened into another cavern. Mark again held his torch high and walked to the center of the room.

Michael touched his torch to Mark's and they could see seven large flat stones arranged in a pattern. Four formed the corners of a rectangle. Three others formed a crooked line from one of the corners.

On the wall at the far end of the cavern were seven animal skulls hanging from leather straps. The boys walked over to them to get a better look. Each skull was stuffed with tundra grass mixed with tar.

"I think these are ceremonial lamps," Mark said and held his torch to one. The light from the skull lamp cast eerie shadows on the walls. Mark held his torch to another. The cavern was bathed in a yellow glow. At the far end of the cavern was another tunnel. On the floor inside the black entrance was the unmistakable skull of a large bear. Black voids were where its eyes should be, yet it seemed to stare at the intruders. Its jaws were open and its fangs shone in the flickering light.

"It's like its guarding the entrance," Mark shouted, his voice echoed into the unknown void. "Let's see where it goes. Get one of the ceremonial lamps just in case we need it."

Michael hesitantly did as he was asked and followed Mark.

Mark glanced down as he carefully stepped over the skull. He caught his breath. On the skull were seven yellow spots. Four formed the corners of a rectangle and three more formed a crooked line off one corner.

He thought of the pouch Granddad had given him, "It's just like ..." He stopped and pointed the torch at the unknown void in front of them. "Come on Michael."

The boys continued for some distance. The tunnel veered to their left. They could no longer see the glow of the skull lamps in the cavern behind them. The stale air made them breathe a little harder. The only sound was the scrape of their mukluks on the stone floor and the occasional hiss of the burning torch. Mark held his flame high. There was no trace of black soot on the ceiling of the cave. They were now explorers in uncharted territory.

The cave veered to their right and split into two tunnels. Michael said, "Do you think we should go back?"

"No let's go a little farther. Use that piece of flint and scratch a line on the wall. That'll mark our way."

The cave turned to the left and again split into two tunnels, one not as tall or wide as the other. Mark chose the larger branch and continued. He had the feeling they were walking downhill. Michael continued to mark their path. Another twenty steps and the cave branched to the left and right. They took the right tunnel. Michael looked behind them. A few feet outside the flame was total darkness. Ahead was the black unknown. Michael cocked his head. Mark heard it too. Water dripping. Mark held his torch to the side. The wall and floor of the cave were wet.

A few steps more and the tunnel suddenly widened into a cavern bigger than the one they first entered. The boys hugged the narrow rim along the left wall. Mark's torch was burning a dull orange and smoking profusely.

"Give me the skull lamp. This one's had it." Mark touched the torch to the lamp and it sprung to life casting a light which reflected off the strange setting. He dropped his torch. It hissed when it hit the water on the cave floor and went out.

The scene before them was from another world. Rocks shaped like long wet spikes hung dripping from the ceiling; others grew from the floor, pointing upward. It reminded Mark of the open jaws of a pre-historic monster.

"Wow, that's awesome," was all Michael could say.

Everything was wet and dripping as they made their way along the edge of the cavern. The floor was now quite slippery. The boys' mukluks made splashing sounds as they carefully made their way forward.

The cave branched again. They took the left branch. Fifteen steps ahead a small tunnel appeared on their right. They stayed in the larger one. The water on the cave floor was now an inch deep and running in the direction they were going. The cave narrowed and the ceiling got lower. The boys had to walk crouched over. Mark's back began to ache from his bent-over position. His leg muscles throbbed.

The flame of Michael's torch began to turn orange and smoke. Mark thought, *Can we possibly find our way back if we loose our light?*

Michael said in a low voice, "Mark."

"I know. We'll be okay."

Michael's torch flickered and went out.

Mark held the skull lamp in front of him. Absolute darkness surrounded them except for the flame from the skull. The tunnel was so narrow it brushed Mark's shoulders. He turned them slightly to keep from rubbing the wet walls. All of the muscles in Mark's body ached as he moved forward in a twisted position holding their only light. The cave widened abruptly and turned to the left.

Mark lost his footing and fell backward. His head hit the watery floor with a thunk. He gasped for breath. The last thing he saw was the fear in Michael's face as the skull lamp skidded along the floor, turned over and went out with a hiss. Total blackness crushed around them. The only sounds were the drip, drip from the cave walls and the boy's heavy breathing.

Michael said in a fear stressed voice, "Mark are you okay. Say something. I don't know where you ..."

"Yeah, okay," Mark wheezed. He lay outstretched on the cave floor. Icy water ran down the neck of his shirt and into his wool trousers. Mark could taste stale musty air. He sat up in the moving water on the cave floor.

"Just give me a minute." He got to his knees. He heard a voice in his mind, *Never give up. Move onward.*

"I can't see anything. Mark? Where are you?"

Mark took off the leather belt tied around his waist. "I'm here. Michael. Take hold of my belt." Mark swung his belt in an arc waist high. It hit something.

"That was me," Michael said. Mark swung it again and Michael caught it.

"Tie your belt to it and hold on."

"How will we know which way to go?"

Mark had an idea. He lowered his hand to the cave floor and felt the running water. "This way," as he got to his feet and he gently tugged on the belt. He held out his arm and kept his hand on the side of the wet cave.

"Put your hand on the wall. It will help you keep your balance."

They inched along. The only sounds were the splashing of their mukluks on the watery floor and the dripping from the cave walls.

Our guide is the running water at our feet, Mark told himself,

A few more small steps. At first Mark thought he was seeing things. A dim glow. Up ahead.

He stopped. Listened. He thought he could hear gurgling. They moved ahead a few more steps. The cave suddenly widened. Mark stopped as the floor ended at a glowing pool of water. It seemed brighter to their left than to the right. They could see the wet walls glistening on the other side. This was the end of the tunnel.

At their feet water was running off the cave floor, making a gurgling sound as it drained into the glowing pool.

Mark stared at the dim light, "You know what? See how the pool is darker there than it is here? And see how the water runs into the pool and doesn't backup on the cave floor? Mark could barely see Michael's silhouette but he thought he could see him nod.

"Yeah, I do. I understand."

"Are you ready?"

"Yes."

Mark took a deep breath, held his nose and jumped into the pool. Michael followed. The water was icy cold. They swam downward, then toward the light, then upward and broke the surface of the water into the sunlight outside the walls of the cave.

Mark sputtered, thrashed his arms and looked to see where Michael was.

Mark's Mom turned around in her seat, "You two settle down back there. We've barely gotten started and we have a long ride ahead of us."

The boys looked at each other and grinned.

CHAPTER SIX

THE PHONE CALL

The rest of the ride was uneventful. Dad stopped at Michael's house and dropped him off.

Michael smiled, "Thanks for asking me to go along. I had a great time. See you at school." Michael bounded up his steps and opened the front door.

Dad put the car in gear and continued home. He looked in the rearview mirror, "Looks like you've a good friend."

Mark nodded. He thought about the excitement and adventures they had. He held the box Granddad gave him in his lap. I wonder what's in the envelope. I'll check it when I get home and find a safe place for the pouch and the bear, he told himself.

Dad pulled into their driveway. He and Mark unpacked the car while Mom went inside to start dinner.

Mark went to his room and got his shoebox from the closet. He took the letter out of the box Granddad gave him and put the leather pouch with the ivory bear in the shoebox beside his baseball cards and on top of the grizzly's

57

claw.

He closed the lid and put it back on the shelf. Mark set the envelope on his bed to read later and went downstairs.

The phone rang just as Mark and his mom and dad were sitting down to dinner. Mom had made Mark's favorite, a pot roast cooked with potatoes and carrots. He was hungry and disappointed by the phone's interruption.

Mom answered, "Hello."

She didn't say another word. She listened for a moment and handed the phone to Dad.

He said, "Hello. How bad is it?" He listened for a long time. "Where are you now?" His face stiffened. "Would you like me to ..? Are you sure? Alright, but call us when you know anything more." His voice was almost a whisper, "Okay, we'll wait. Goodbye."

He handed the phone to Mom and sat silent for a moment. Dad's eyes were glassy. He stared blankly at the table and his voice cracked, "Granddad collapsed in the garage. The paramedics think it's his heart. They took him to Saint Elizabeth's Hospital. He's in intensive care and..." Dad took a deep breath, "He's not conscious. They're watching him very closely."

Mom put her hand on Dad's, "Do you think..."

Dad interrupted, "They said it was best to wait until they know more." He tried to force a smile, slowly got up and went into the living room. The roast went untouched.

Later, Mark heard his mom cleaning up the kitchen. He sat on his bed and picked up the envelope, opened it and read.

Mark,

It is time to tell you more about the ivory bear. Only you and I share its secret. I was chosen with its safekeeping for reasons I don't understand. I remember now that the Eskimo who carved it told me it was special and not like his other carvings. I didn't know what he meant at the time but I have since learned.

Only its keeper and the first son of his first son may know its power. It is just a carving to others.

The bear took me many places over the years. I now know they were tests to see if the keeper of the bear was prepared to answer the call when needed. Should it come it will be from the elders of seven Alaskan tribes. I'm told you are almost ready.

If they call it will be a very important matter. You can accept or decline but I would encourage you to think seriously about your decision.

You can always call to me and I will answer. The future will not change that. You are now the keeper of the bear.

Use its power wisely,

Granddad

The next morning the house was quiet. Mark woke just before his clock went off, dressed for school and went downstairs. Mom was in the kitchen.

He asked, "Did we get a call about Granddad?"

"Dad went to the hospital."

Just then the phone rang. It was Dad and she put it on speaker. "How is he doing?"

"Granddad passed away during the night. He never regained consciousness. I'm going to stay here awhile and then bring Grandmother home with me. Be there soon."

Mom began to cry. School was out of the question.

CHAPTER SEVEN

THIEVES IN THE NIGHT

Mark had no way to know that his second world was also about to make a dramatic change. It was the night of the full moon and four shadowy figures crouched in the snow covered tundra at the edge of a Yup'ik village on the Kuskokwim Delta of southwestern Alaska. A fifth with eyes the color of night stared at the ring of log houses built around the Gasqiq or council lodge. Smoke slowly curled from the sleeping fires of the cabins sending lazy spirals into the cold night air. From a distance the coalescing smoke shimmered in the moon's reflection giving the appearance that someone or something had scrawled a warning across the midnight sky.

The Gasqiq, made of cedar logs, in the center of the village, was much larger than the natives' cabins. It was a meeting place where the men of the Yup'ik spoke to the animal world, the earth and the sea as their fathers had done and their fathers before them. It was important to the village to speak to the spirits of nature.

The council lodge was the place used to make important decisions and perform the ceremonial dances. It was here the elders passed the legends of the village to the younger men. It was here they wore the spirit robes, dancing masks and feathers of the golden eagle. It was here chants were sung to the slow tharum of skin drums.

The intruders knew well the value of the lodge to the Yup'ik and of the ceremonial treasures within. The motive was clear for the one with eyes the color of night. He wished to punish the village for driving him away. The council had ruled that he must leave for angering the animal spirits. Should he remain, the village believed it would severely suffer.

He joined other outcasts from other villages. Four now stood outside the council lodge. The Yup'ik outcast moved quietly toward the outer ring of cabins, his silver gray coat shone in the moonlight, his head was covered by a black fur hood. He paused scanning the familiar scene of his childhood. Now after eighteen winters he had no home and anger burned in his heart. He would have revenge. He would show no mercy.

The outcast crept to the low entrance of the ceremonial lodge. As he advanced forward so did his companions, then they crouched again in the snow, awaiting his next move. The outcast stepped inside the lodge. The only evidence of his presence was the trail of footprints in the snow.

In the glow of dying embers in the fire circle in the center of the room he could see the deer skin dancing robes decorated with colorful beads hanging on the wall. He saw the headdresses and ceremonial masks made of skin and wood, feathers and ivory. And then he saw, hanging in its special place, illuminated by the embers glow, the necklace of the bear spirit. It was made of claw and teeth, strips of fur and small pieces of carved ivory. He knew the power it held for the village and that only the highest elder was allowed to wear it and only during the ceremony of the great bear.

The outcast seemed nervous as he approached it. Perhaps it was the punishment he was about to unleash on the village. He pulled it from its special place and the necklace fell.

As it struck the ground the Yup'ik elder in a nearby cabin was awakened by a sharp pain. The elder pushed back his sleeping robe and put a hand to the burning spot on his chest. He found nothing wrong yet it hurt as though he were severely wounded. With a grimace of pain on his wrinkled face he looked around in the dim light of his sleeping fire to find nothing disturbed in his one room cabin.

From nearby he heard the howl of a wolf. He slowly got to his feet and stepped outside. The elder caught his breath in the sharp cold and saw in the moonlight, the one who had been driven from the village.

The outcast stood beside the entrance of the Gasqiq. He was clutching something under his arm and ran to the edge of the clearing. The elder shouted a warning, "Tig-luk-tuk-tuk, thieves steal."

Men swarmed out of their cabins, some

carried bows, some carried rifles. There was excitement, shouting and confusion. One of the thieves fired his weapon from the edge of the clearing. A Yup'ik villager fell. He would rise no more. The snow he lay on turned crimson.

Each intruder mounted a snowmobile and clutched an arm to his chest as though he held that which was stolen. Each drove his snowmobile in a different direction and disappeared into the night.

The men of the village fired weapons but to no avail. It would not be until the next morning that they would discover what had been stolen. If the necklace of the bear spirit was not returned, the village believed everyone in it would die. So was the legend. The men of the Yup'ik set out. There were trails to follow.

CHAPTER EIGHT

CALL TO THE ELDERS

The thieves had a long lead. They were strong and swift. Each took a separate path. Yet each headed for a common destination. Many days went by. The hunters and the hunted crossed the river's delta, then northward onto rolling slopes covered with thorny devil's club and white willow. On they traveled along the bank of the Yukon River then east into hemlock and cedar forests where the trails were lost. The Yup'ik hunters wearily returned home. They must find another way.

Alone the Yup'ik village elder entered the Gasqiq and lighted a small fire of black spruce cones and branches of the salmonberry bush. Smoke rose. He stared into the curling vapors and sang a chant to the bear spirit. A call for help.

Days went by, then on the day of the new moon, in a snowy clearing on Mount Alyeska in the Chugach Mountains of southern Alaska, seven elders from seven tribes gathered and sat in a council circle under the cold midnight sky.

In the center were seven burning oil lamps, four formed the corners of a rectangle and three more formed a crooked line off one corner. The lamps were placed in the pattern of the Big Dipper, the body of Ursa Major, the Great Bear. Each elder stared upward, eyes fixed upon the starry constellation. All wore a robe of an Alaskan bear, six brown, one white. Each elder extended his arms, palms opened toward the stars and slowly repeated a chant. They spoke in their own tongues, Inuit, Yup'ik, Aleut, Koyukon, Inupiaq, Tlingit and Kolchan.

Then the elder in the white robe spoke in Inupiat to the sky, "Spirit of Bear help get back what thief in wolf skin has taken. If not returned all in the village of the Yup'ik will die."

The elders lowered their eyes and stared at the seven burning lamps. First, the lamp pointing to the North Star began to flicker and smoke, then another and another. A wispy white cloud coalesced above the seven lamps. The form of someone unrecognized by them appeared in the gossamer haze.

Each elder slowly beat a skin drum, Tha-rum, Tha-rum and chanted to the spirit of the Great Bear. Their frosty breaths could be seen in the dark of the night.

The elder in the fur of the white bear spoke to the others, "Travel your lands and search for one seen in smoke of lamps. He hunt killer of Yup'ik. He hunt one in wolf robe. He bring necklace of bear to rightful place. Meet again when moon is new."

Each nodded, raised their arms toward the stars and disappeared into the night. The north wind howled. There was no trace in the snow.

CHAPTER NINE

NEW MOON

The Alaskan moon grew to its fullest and began to wane. The night of the new moon arrived. The elders reappeared as if by magic in the black of night and sat around the lamps as they had before. The Inupiat Elder, Weeok, in the fur of the white bear spoke again to the others, "Name the one who will hunt the killers of men and thieves who steal from Yup'ik people.

The Yup'ik elder replied, "People say Marktok who hunt whale."

The Tlingit spoke, "Marktok who face ash from burning mountain."

Then the Koyukon, "Marktok who save friend in winter forest."

The Aleut called out, "Marktok, who fight bear with fiery torch."

The Kolchan said, "Marktok, caribou hunter."

The Inuit added, "Marktok, who hunt seal on sea of ice."

Then each Elder beat a skin drum and in many tongues chanted,

"We call Marktok to
hunt thief who wear
skin of black head
wolf and those who
join him.
Marktok, hear
call."

The elder in the fur of the white bear
raised his hand. Each tribal leader rose and
stepped into the pattern of lamps. They placed
their hands on the outstretched hand of the
leader Weeok. The flames flickered and white
smoke billowed encircling their knees.

In the northern sky shimmering light could
be seen. Flashing pastels of green and yellow,
pink and white. The Aurora, the Northern Lights,
in the heavens, grew brighter. The colors
undulated and danced along the horizon. The
elders took this as a sign from the spirit of the
sky.

The Elder Weeok in white fur said, "Hear
us Marktok. Let bear grow cold in your hand.
People of Weeok await."

CHAPTER TEN

HEARING THE CALL

Mark woke with a start from a sound sleep. He looked around the darkened room. The bedroom door was open and he could see a nightlight dimly illuminating the hallway. He slowly sat up.

He remembered Dad had brought Grandmother home from the hospital to stay with them. Mark, like the rest of the family, felt a great sadness and loss. He couldn't believe Granddad was gone.

There was no sound in the house. The others were still asleep. He shivered though it was not cold and he was now wide awake. Mark looked at the clock. The lighted red numbers read 5:45.

I guess I just dreamed someone called my name, he thought as he sat in the dark.

Mark swung his legs over the side of the bed and stood. Slowly he walked to the door and stepped into the hallway. All the other bedroom doors were closed. He walked to the top of the stairway and looked down then turned.

Nothing unusual, he told himself. He walked back to his room and could see a dull yellow glow along the bottom of the closet door. "That's strange," he whispered.

Mark eased the door open. The glow was coming from a shelf. Coming from his shoebox. He got the box down, set it on his desk and slowly raised the lid. The glow came from the seven spots on the pouch containing the ivory bear. Unconsciously Mark lifted it out. He studied the pattern but saw something different in his mind. It was an Eskimo elder, arms raised, palms facing outward.

Mark didn't hear the elder but heard a different and familiar voice, *"The Alaskan Elders and the People of Weeok call for your help. How do you answer?"*

Mark was shocked and whispered, "Granddad?"

The voice replied, *"You are ready. I will be near."*

The decision was his. Mark didn't hesitate. He raised his other hand and wrapped his fingers around the pouch holding the ivory bear.

He heard the wind, felt the cold, saw darkness, felt warmth, the smell of fresh cut cedar. He sensed his feet touch bare earth.

Tha-rum, tha-rum. Mark's vision began to clear. He was in a large log building and was not alone.

Through a haze he could see men sitting on the floor around him. Each was slowly beating a skin drum.

Lamps encircled him. They were set out in some sort of pattern. Mark smelled the pungent aroma of burning seal oil. The smoke from the flickering flames spread across the floor, covering his ankles giving the appearance he was standing on a cloud.

Each in the circle of men was chanting and each spoke in a different tongue.

Mark looked at the wrinkled faces and dark eyes of the circle of elders. He counted. There were seven. Each elder's long gray hair was tied behind him. They wore deer skin trousers tied at the waist with a strip of rawhide decorated with colored shells. Their chests, arms and feet were bare.

Mark slowly turned realizing that he too was dressed like those in the circle. In his hand he held a rawhide necklace. Attached to it was the single claw of the grizzly he received from Blacky Rustov on Kodiak Island. He glanced down and saw on his chest, the four scars he got from the claws of the polar bear on the sea of ice.

The circle of elders stared at the place where Mark stood but appeared not to see him. Mark looked around the room. It was made of logs and had a high ceiling with a round hole in the center for smoke to escape from the ceremonial fires. On the walls he saw deer skin dancing robes decorated with colorful shells. He saw the headdresses and ceremonial masks made of skin and wood, feathers and ivory.

The floor was bare earth and hard packed from the feet of the ceremonial dances. Mark had read about such a place. A place for only the men of the village.

One of the Elders put down his skin drum and stood. He walked toward Mark, seeming to glide across the smoke covered floor. He held a seal skin pouch. The drums grew louder. Dum, dum, tha-rum, tha-rum. The flickering oil lamps cast moving shadows on the elder's face. He stood in front of Mark.

Mark recognized the face, the Inupiat Elder Weeok and stared into his dark eyes. The elder did not speak. The drums stopped. The lodge was silent, damp and warm. Beads of sweat ran down Mark's back.

Weeok took the bear claw necklace Mark was holding and placed it around Mark's neck. Then the Elder opened the pouch and took out a small container made of woven baleen from Arviq, the whale. He dipped two fingers into the soft mixture in the jar.

Weeok said, "Blue clay from volcanoes to south. Ground bark from totem spruce to east. Bearberry and marsh fleawort from tundra far north, oil from seal of western sea. So saying Weeok painted each scar on Marks chest with the mixture.

Mark looked down at the four blue streaks. He drew a deep breath. His scars felt hot. Weeok took a feather of the golden eagle from his belt and dipped the quill tip into the jar.

He touched Mark's forehead seven times forming the pattern of the Big Dipper, the body of the constellation of the great bear. Weeok placed the jar and pouch down. They disappeared in the layer of white smoke covering their ankles.

The Elder Weeok again broke the silence of the lodge, "You answer bear spirit's call. From this time you be Marktok-of-Nanuk, Mark-of-the-Bear. All villages will know. You hunt thief who wear skin of black head wolf and return necklace of great bear to its place in Yup'ik Gasgiq."

Mark held out his open hands and said in a low voice, "But I have no weapons for such a hunt."

The six seated on the floor began a slow soft beat. Dum, dum, tha-rum as the Inupiat Elder Weeok leaned toward Mark, "We give you what you need. Tell you what you must know."

The seven oil lamps flickered. The Elder of the Yup'ik arose and walked to the wall. He took a handmade spear from its rest and grasped it with both hands. He held the red, black and blue painted spear with a sharpened bone tip above his head. The Yup'ik elder stood beside Weeok.

The layer of white smoke rose to Mark's knees, his waist, above his head. It rose until it disappeared through the hole in the ceiling.

The Elder Weeok spoke. "Let hunt begin."

GLOSSARY

Alaskan husky -- A dog used by Alaskan natives as a work animal for such things as pulling a sled or carrying a pack.

http://www.flickr.com/photos/quoimedia/5403502096/

Alaskan Wolf -- Carnivorous predator which hunts game in groups called packs. This variety lives predominantly in central and southern Alaska.

Photo by Jan Nijendijk.5097CC BY-SA 3.0

Chert -- Sedimentary rock made of micro crystalline silica. Dark colored varieties are called flint

Dog sled -- :a sled pulled by one or more dogs used to travel over ice and through snow.
Dog power has been used for hunting and travel for hundreds of years in Alaska.

Eskimos -- (Es-ki-mos) Groups of people native to the polar region. More appropriately called Inupiat (Western Arctic), Yup'ik (Western-central Alaska), Inuit (Eastern Arctic), etc.

Inuit man

Hemlock trees -- common in central and southern Alaska. It is a conifer which means it has seed cones as do pine and spruce trees.

Mukluk -- (muk-luk) Traditionally a soft boot made of caribou or sealskin.

under the Creative Commons Attribution-Share Alike 2.5 Generic *license*

Qana: (ka-na) There are many words in Alaskan native languages which describe snow. This one refers to falling snow

Snowshoe -- A wooden frame webbed with raw hide. Used by Native Alaskans to walk on loose or under compacted snow.

Free Art License
(http://commons.wikimedia.org/wiki/Category:FAL)

Spruce tree -- a conifer, which means it has seed cones as do pine trees. Common in southern and central Alaska

http://creativecommons.org/licenses/by-sa/3.0/

Totem pole (Alaska): Carved by Native Alaskans. They represent animals or plants that serves as an emblem of a group of **people**, such as a clan, group, lineage, or tribe, reminding them of their ancestry (or mythic past)

(http://creativecommons.org/licenses/by/2.0/)

Ursa Major -- A constellation called the Great Bear. It includes the Big Dipper also known as the Body of the Great Bear

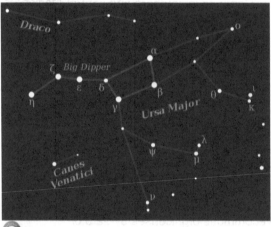

http://commons.wikimedia.org/wiki/User:Rursus

LEAVE A REVIEW

Please take this occasion to leave your opinion about BODY OF THE GREAT BEAR if you thought other readers would enjoy it. Readers and writers rely on reviews. Your opinion will help others make future reading decisions.

Here's how to leave a comment on Amazon.com:
Either go to my webpage (ralambauthor.com) then click the button beside the book cover on my Books Page which reads CLICK TO FIND ON AMAZON   or   go directly to Amazon.com and do a book title search. Enter (BODY OF THE GREAT BEAR) in the search bar.
To the right of the stars on the book page you will see the number of customer reviews. Click on the words (customer reviews) This will take you to the review page. Click the button (Create your own review)
Enter a rating and a brief comment
Click SUBMIT

CONTACT ME

Get the latest information on new releases at my website:
HTTP://ralambauthor.com

Send your comments on: Twitter at HTTP://twitter.com/RA_Lamb or follow me on Facebook at HTTP://www.facebook.com/Robert.Lamb.96199 or Email to ralamb@ralambauthor.com

ABOUT THE AUTHOR

The episodes and characters in this book are fictional; however, the settings are based on personal experiences. Not only has the author set foot in every place depicted but during his youth he also changed schools several times and had to face up more than once as the new kid on the block.

R.A. writes YA and Middle Grade adventure stories although he has written several picture books for younger children and a few nonfiction pieces.

He strives to supply sufficient description to let you the reader feel you are in the midst of the fantasy as it unfolds, but beware, not all paths are predictable. What's the fun of living in the story if everything leads to the obvious?

He and his wife live in the Woodlands, Texas near Houston.

A PERSONAL WORD FROM THE AUTHOR

I hope you enjoyed this book as much as I did writing it and will follow the continuation of Mark's adventures in Book Three, MARK OF THE BEAR coming soon.

ACKNOWLEDGEMENTS

I thank my family, my writers critique group and my friends for their support.

Finally I would like to thank my proof readers, David Maier and Kim O'Brein who found the typos and made wording suggestions which made this a better book.

RIGHTS

This book is a work of fiction. Names, characters and incidents are either products of the author's imagination or used fictitiously. Any similarity to actual people, organizations, and/or events is purely coincidental.

Made in United States
Troutdale, OR
01/04/2025

27632458R00050